Dr. H Explores the Universe
©Unapologetically Being, Inc. 2017

Cover Artist Patrick Giles
Sketch Artist Derek J. Luke

Published in the United States of America

Unapologetically Being, Inc.
3157 Gentilly Blvd Suite #2029
New Orleans, LA 70122
985-236-1913

Website: www.unapologeticallybeing.org
Email: Contact@unapologeticallybeing.org

ISBN: 978-0-9993512-2-2 Limited Edition Hardback
ISBN: 978-0-9993512-0-8 Hardback
ISBN: 978-0-9993512-1-5 Paperback

Limited Edition Hardback Published 2017
Hardback Published 2017
Paperback Published 2017

This book is dedicated to changing the face of Science, Technology, Engineering and Math while fighting illiteracy one story at a time.

Dedicated to Gabriel, who will live out my legacy.

Thank you Eric, Malik, and Denise for your support and living in my legacy.

Thank you Christian for pushing me.

-K. Renee Horton, Ph.D.

Grace,
Thank you for
your support!

Dr. H

Author: K Renee Horton, Ph.D

Dr. RENEÉ EXPLORES THE UNIVERSE
FROM MERCURY TO MARS

Artist: Patrick Giles   Sketch Artist: Derek J. Luke

While most people loved to have adventures on Earth, Dr. H wanted to explore somewhere far more exciting. Her purple VW beetle named Bouchet Beetle, BB for short, had a magical ability that no one else knew about. BB was excellent at driving on roads, but it could also travel in space!

Dr. H was ready to have a space adventure, so she hopped into BB, and they whooshed straight in the air. They traveled through Earth's ozone layer and were soon surrounded by billions of stars in all directions.

"Where should we go first?" Dr. H asked as she sat in the driver's seat.

"Why don't we visit the planets today?" BB suggested, and she liked the idea.

BB turned around and sped towards Mercury, which was the closest planet to the sun. It looked similar to Earth's moon, rocky and covered head to toe with craters.

Dr. H began to sweat the closer they traveled to Mercury since it was the Sun's neighbor. She slipped into her astronaut suit as BB landed on the surface.

She hopped out and BB drove beside her as they explored the planet.

Dr. H grabbed a handful of sandy rubble off the ground and held it on her flat palm. It didn't fly away even a little.

"That's so fascinating!" she exclaimed. "Mercury has no atmosphere, so there's no wind or weather of any kind."

They approached a wide crater as BB had an exciting idea. He drove up to the edge and smiled at Dr. H.

"The crater looks like a ramp. Hop onto my roof, Dr. H!" he exclaimed as she hopped on.

BB drove down the crater as they sped towards the center. They swooshed across and drove up the other side. But inside of driving out, BB performed a somersault in midair as they drove back across the crater. Dr. H held on tight as she enjoyed the fun ride.

"Since Mercury has much less mass than Earth, the gravity isn't so strong! We weigh about one-third of our normal weight here!" BB explained excitedly.

After several flips, BB drove out of the crater as they went on a bumpy ride. The surface was quite rocky, so Dr. H hopped up and down on the roof.

"BB, can you guess how long a year is on Mercury?" Dr. H asked with a sly smile.

"I know Earth has 365 days, but I have no idea about Mercury."

"There are only two days in the entire year!"

BB couldn't believe it. Only two days in the year? It seemed so short, but it was true.

When the pair was ready to move on, Dr. H hopped back inside as BB flew over to the next planet. Venus was next in line and the brightest planet in the solar system. If you knew where to look, you could see Venus in the sky from Earth.

They traveled through thick clouds and landed on the surface to find the gravity just like Earth. BB wouldn't be able to do any fancy tricks in the air. Dr. H hopped out to find themselves surrounded by active volcanos!

Wherever there wasn't a volcano was a deep crater. The planet looked like a stormy desert. Since Venus had such thick cloud, there was almost no sunshine on the surface of the planet. It was dark and murky.

Dr. H was already sweating in her astronaut suit, which made her giggle. At least there would be a little bit of water on Venus since the planet didn't have any to start with.

"Do you want to play Lava, BB?" Dr. H asked as he grinned widely.

Dr. H hopped back onto BB's roof as they drove around the planet. Like the kid's game of Lava, BB and Dr. H tried to avoid the flowing lava and wide cracks on the planet. BB flew above the lava and landed once they cleared it.

"Lava to our left!" Dr. H warned as BB hopped off the surface and flew above the lava. He was about to land when he spotted a wide crack. BB sped up and landed safely on the other side of it. "Phew, that was close!"

They had a fun time playing Lava, but it was time to move on. Dr. H plopped back inside BB as they flew back into space. Earth was the next planet in the solar system, but since it was home, they decided to zip right past it and travel to Mars.

Mars was known as the Red Planet because it had a red dusty and rocky surface. They landed easily as they began to explore the planet. Dr. H pointed to a wide canyon to their left that spanned far into the distance.

"Scientists think that canyons like these were created by water a long time ago," Dr. H explained.

"I didn't think Mars had any water."

"The polar ice caps actually have thin layers of ice," Dr. H stated.

But before they could explore any further, they suddenly heard a strange howling noise. They couldn't put their finger on it until they spotted a massive dust storm approaching in the distance. Mars was known for their sand storms.

"Do you want to go for a Mars sand storm, Dr. H?" BB asked hopefully. It sounded like a lot of fun.

"Let's do it!"

Dr. H hopped back inside as BB drove straight at the sand storm. When they were close enough, they were swept into the air and twirled around and around. Dr. H and BB shouted excitedly like they were on an amusement park ride.

The sand storm continued to spin them around the planet as Dr. H pointed out the window.

They continued to travel with the sand storm until they grew a bit nauseous. BB flew out of the sand storm and back out to space. Dr. H's tummy began to grumble, so they decided it was time to go back home.

She slipped out of her astronaut suit and relaxed in the driver's seat as BB flew her back to Earth. She was excited to continue their space adventure next time because Pluto was her favorite planet. They had a long way to go to meet it.

THE END...UNTIL THE NEXT ADVENTURE, DR. H EXPLORES THE UNIVERSE - JUPITER TO URANUS.

CPSIA information can be obtained
at www.ICGtesting.com
Printed in the USA
LVIC06n0825280218
568090LV00001B/11